THOMAS & FRIENDS™

The Snow Special

Based on
The Railway Series
by the
Rev. W. Awdry

Illustrations by
Robin Davies

EGMONT

We bring stories to life

First published in Great Britain in 2017
by Egmont UK Limited
The Yellow Building, 1 Nicholas Road, London W11 4AN

Thomas the Tank Engine & Friends™

CREATED BY BRITT ALLCROFT

HiT entertainment

ISBN 978 1 4052 8771 5
67245/1
Printed in Italy

Written by Emily Stead. Designed by Claire Yeo.
Series designed by Martin Aggett.

FSC
MIX
Paper
FSC® C018306

When snow came to Sodor,
Henry was the only engine who
didn't get stuck. He thought his
trucks must be lucky! But
how would Henry get on
without his lucky trucks?

Winter had arrived on Sodor, and the Island was covered with snow.

The tracks were icy and slippery, and many of the lines were blocked by snowdrifts.

Henry puffed happily through the snowy countryside. None of **his** lines were blocked!

Henry was the first engine to arrive back at the Sheds that evening. All his friends were late!

Thomas rolled in next. "Well done, Henry," he chuffed. "You must have lucky trucks!"

"Maybe you're right, Thomas!" Henry smiled.

And Henry went to sleep, feeling proud of his lucky trucks.

But the next morning, Henry's lucky trucks weren't in the Yard. Henry gasped!

"Edward took your trucks," Thomas explained. "He's delivering coal to the villages."

The Fat Controller arrived. "A delivery of presents is waiting at the Airport," he told Henry. "You must take a gift to all the children in the villages."

Henry set off nicely, but the rails at Gordon's Hill were very slippery.

Every time Henry tried to puff up the hill, he slid back down! It took a long time to reach the top.

"I need my lucky trucks!" Henry worried. "I must find Edward right away."

Henry steamed on through the snow. But soon he had to stop. Some logs had rolled off James' flatbed and were blocking Henry's way.

"Bust my buffers!" cried Henry. "This would never have happened if I'd had my lucky trucks!"

"You should be at the Airport!" James snorted.

"Not without my lucky trucks," Henry replied. "I must find Edward first."

Henry set off slowly. His wheels **slipped** and **slid** on the icy rails, but he kept going.

The more Henry thought about the children, the less he thought about his lucky trucks.

At last, he arrived at the Airport. He collected the presents and puffed away to begin his deliveries.

Henry shivered sadly, while Rocky set to work clearing the track.

"Don't worry, Henry," Rocky rumbled. "You'll soon be on your way!"

Rocky was right! The tracks were quickly cleared and Henry steamed away to find Edward.

But everywhere that Henry chuffed, there were more delays.

"Hurry please, Thomas," Henry wheeshed.
"I need to find Edward and my lucky trucks."

Thomas puffed as quickly as he could to clear the snow, but it was hard work. Henry had to wait.

"I'll never find my lucky trucks," Henry sighed.

But at the Frosty Forest, Henry **did** find his lucky trucks, and Edward too! Henry beamed from buffer to bumper!

He tried to stop but his wheels slid on the icy tracks. Henry crashed straight into the line of trucks! **BASH!**

"My lucky trucks are broken!" Henry cried.

Henry sat sadly in the snow. He didn't want to go anywhere without his lucky trucks.

"But they're broken," said Edward. "And the presents still need collecting."

Henry thought about how sad the children would feel if they didn't have a present to open.

"I must get to the Airport," he puffed. "With or without my lucky trucks!"

Henry steamed all over the Island until he had just one delivery left. Some children were waiting for him at the station.

"Hooray for Henry!" they cheered.

"I didn't need my lucky trucks, after all!" Henry smiled.

And when he looked at the children's smiling faces, he felt like the luckiest engine on Sodor!

tender

cab

dome

smoke box

funnel

coupling hook

boiler band

buffer

Henry's challenge to you

Look back through the pages of this book
and see if you can spot:

bird

snowman

star

presents

red flag

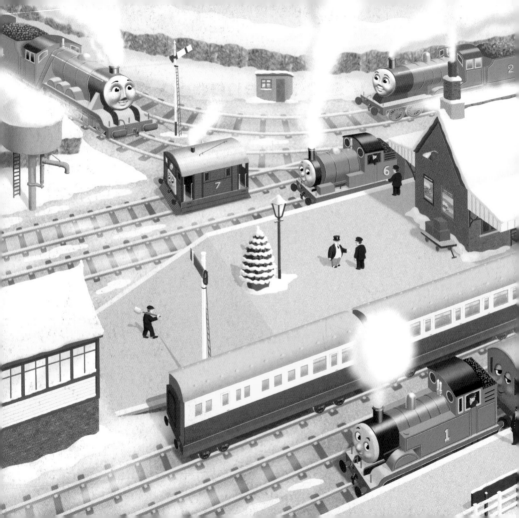